Marks and Spencer Limited
Baker Street, London, England 1428/3000

SBN 361 04704 5
Text and artwork copyright © 1979 Purnell and Sons Limited
Mrs Hedgehog character copyright © 1979 Marks and Spencer Limited
Published September 1979 by Purnell Books, Berkshire House,
Queen Street, Maidenhead, Berkshire
Made and printed in Great Britain by Purnell and Sons Limited,
Paulton (Bristol) and London
Reprinted July 1980, July 1981

St Michael

Tales of

Mrs Hedgehog

Stories by Susannah Bradley

Illustrations by Kate Lloyd-Jones

A Home for Henrietta

O n a bright Spring day in Greenglades Wood, nothing seemed to be stirring, but if you thought that nobody was there, you were wrong. All the creatures would be in hiding if you were clumping around picking primroses in your big, clumsy Wellington boots.

Woodland creatures, you see, are quick to hide themselves

at the least sound of a human approaching. So had you been in Greenglades Wood that morning, you would have glimpsed no more than a wing flutter from Charlie Crow as he swooped overhead, well out of your reach, and you would have had to be sharp-eyed to spot Rosemary Rabbit and her sister Amelia, as they bobbed across the fields to do their weekly shopping.

As for Amanda Mole, the woodland store-keeper, and old Mr Badger – well, you would have to wait a long time to see them at all, for they are shyer than anyone.

"You've got more sense than anyone, Amanda," said Mr Badger, as he bought his weekly bag of humbugs, striped black and white like himself, over her counter. "You and I know that the best time to go about one's business is at night, when everyone else, except Owl, is asleep."

"Quite right," said Amanda. "That's why I run this shop. I can stay here out of the sunshine during opening hours."

As Mr Badger turned to leave, Pippin the Squirrel darted past the shop doorway.

"Just look at that mad squirrel," grumbled Mr Badger. "He's got no sense at all. Do you know, Amanda, sometimes he even dares to take crumbs from human hands? He's a young tearaway and no mistake."

Pippin skipped on past Amanda's shop and took the path to the very edge of the wood. There, where the sunlight shone in

all its glory, he scampered up a tall tree and looked out across
the valley. Below him lay a few farm buildings, where
humans kept some tame animals; but this did not bother
Pippin, who was half-tame himself.

A slight movement among the grass at a tumble-down shed
door made him peer more closely.

"Bless my nibblers," said Pippin to himself. "That looks like
a hedgehog!"

Sure enough, with a twitch of the nose and a scurry of the
back paws, a stout lady hedgehog came towards the tree where

Pippin perched. She was a very neat lady hedgehog, with a flowery apron and matching mob-cap. As she reached the edge of the wood, Pippin scampered down his tree to greet her.

"Hello, there!" he said. "Had a nice winter sleep?"

"I don't know how you know about my winter sleep, young squirrel," said the hedgehog. "But yes, thank you, I have."

"Oh, I sleep through the winter myself," said Pippin. "I'm Pippin. Who are you?"

"I'm Henrietta, Mrs Henrietta Hedgehog," said the newcomer. "Would you happen to know of any good lodging houses around here where I could stay until I find my summer home? There will need to be plenty of room, because I'll be enlarging my family soon and you know how much space you need for a growing family."

Pippin scratched his head and thought hard.

"No, I can't say that I do," he replied. "But come with me and I'm sure that something will turn up."

They walked along in silence for a little while.

"Of course, you could always stay with me," Pippin said. "I've got a very nice apartment, snug and dry, with no humans bothering me."

"It sounds good," said Henrietta. "Where is it?"

Pippin pointed to a large tree a few yards away.

"There!" he said, proudly.

"But how do you get in?" asked Henrietta.

"Through that hole, half way up the trunk," replied Pippin.

"Oh no," said Henrietta, sadly. "That would never do for me. I couldn't climb up there, even with a ladder."

A loud cawing noise overhead made them look up and there was Charlie Crow in the sky above. He swooped down to be introduced to Henrietta.

"Could Henrietta stay with you, Charlie?" asked Pippin. "She needs some lodgings for a while."

"You'd be very welcome, Henrietta," said Charlie, who had a kind heart. "But wouldn't it be rather crowded for all of us? My wife might get sat on. And how would you get up to it?"

Henrietta looked up at the nest high up in the topmost
branches of a tree.

"Dear me, it's out of the question," she said. "Thank you all
the same, Charlie."

"Amanda might have an idea," said Charlie. "We could ask
her. What had you in mind, Henrietta?"

"Somewhere low down," said Henrietta. "And someone who doesn't mind me moving about a lot at night. I do most of my work then, you see."

"Let's call on Mr Badger before we see Amanda," said Pippin. "He's a night creature and he may like to share his sett."

When Mr Badger, already annoyed at being woken up, answered the door to them and heard their request, he told them to run away and pester someone else.

"Certainly not!" he snapped. "I've got nothing against you personally, madam, but I couldn't stand a house full of baby hedgehogs!"

So Pippin took Henrietta to see Amanda.

"I've no room myself to take you in," said Amanda. "All my spare space is taken up with the goods I sell in my shop. But I'll tell you what I'll do. I'll put a notice in my shop window,

and you shall stay to have lunch with me, my dear, while we see if anyone answers our advertisement."

Soon a large notice, saying "LODGINGS WANTED BY RESPECTABLE LADY HEDGEHOG AND FAMILY" was propped up in the window, and Amanda and Henrietta were eating ants' eggs on toast in the back kitchen, while getting to know one another.

"This seems a very nice area," said Henrietta. "Nice and quiet to bring a family up in."

"Oh, it is," said Amanda. "My two lads are quiet types and town life just wouldn't suit them. My husband's away a lot, you know, down the mines. Where's yours?"

"I'm a widow," said Henrietta. "My Horace was always one for taking risks. He would keep crossing roads. I said to him, Horace, it's not safe, and it wasn't. One of those big, noisy things came hurtling along one day and that was it. So I'm on my own now, until my babies come."

"How sad," said Amanda. "Still, you'll find some good friends in Greenglades Wood. Pippin and the others will help you build your summer home."

The shop bell tinkled and Amanda scurried into the shop to see what was wanted.

Rosemary and Amelia Rabbit stood there.

"Hope you don't mind . . ." began Amelia.

"But about the lodgings . . ." went on Rosemary.

"For the lady hedgehog . . ." said Amelia.

"We've got some!" finished Rosemary.

Henrietta, hearing this, came through into the shop.

"Have you really?" she said. "I wonder – it's not in a tree, is it? Only that's all I've been offered so far."

"Dear me, no!" said Rosemary quickly. "It's our old burrow,

the one we don't use any more. It's much too big for us but it would be just right for a family."

"Let's go and see it!" said Henrietta.

In the end, everyone went along out of curiosity, even old Mr Badger.

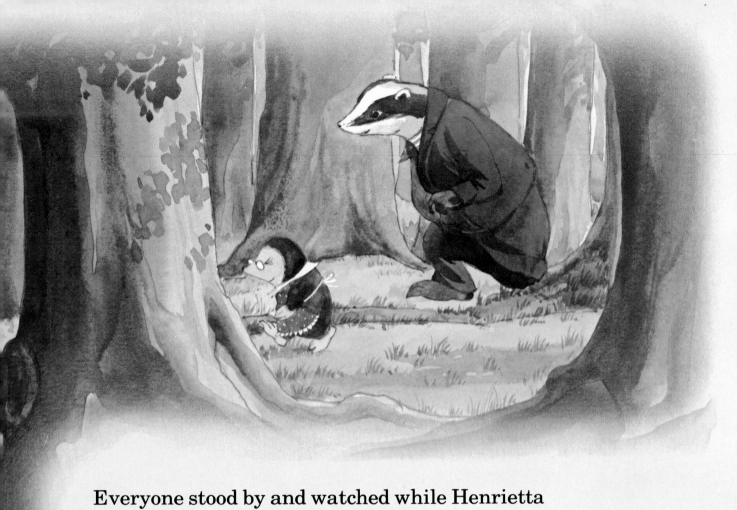

Everyone stood by and watched while Henrietta
disappeared down one hole and came up by another.

"Front and back entrance!" said Pippin.
"Lovely front porch!" said Amanda.
"Nicely secluded," said Charlie Crow.

"It's delightful," said Henrietta. "I'll take it. How much is the rent?"

"What? Oh, no rent," said Amelia.

"Just let us come and play with your babies in the summer," said Rosemary. "We love babies, and we haven't any ourselves."

"Oh thank you!" said Henrietta.

Then, much to everyone's surprise, grumpy, old Mr Badger,

who had walked away some time before, came up to them,
dragging a large bag of leaves.

"Sorry I was rude to you, my dear," he said to Henrietta.
"Here are some things to make your new home more cosy. I

hope you'll be very happy with us here in Greenglades Wood."

"Hear, hear!" cried everyone.

So Henrietta knew that she was going to enjoy living in
Greenglades Wood.

The Baby Hedgehogs' Party

It was a bright, sun-dappled day in Greenglades Wood. Although it was warm enough for a bit of sunbathing, if that was what you wanted, it was not too far into summer for the bluebells to have withered or the grass to have turned yellow from lack of rain. The little group of woodland animals who were gathered under the awning outside Amanda Mole's grocery store did not look very happy, however.

In fact, anyone could see that they looked worried.

They stood in a circle while five baby hedgehogs played around them.

"She said she'd only be ten minutes, and that was nearly an

hour ago," said Amanda Mole from the shop doorway. "I promised to keep an eye on her little ones, for she's minded mine like a good neighbour when my shop's been very busy on a Saturday."

"I'm worried," said old Mr Badger grumpily, having been woken from his daytime snooze in his basement flat by the noise his neighbours were making above. "It's not like Henrietta Hedgehog to travel far from home during the daytime, especially with the little ones. She's usually got more sense, like me, and only goes out at night."

"We should send out a search party," suggested Rosemary Rabbit.

Just then, Charlie Crow came flying down through trees, landing beside them with an excited flutter.

"She's coming! She's coming!" he croaked. "She's just round the bend in the path!"

All the creatures turned to look and sure enough, Henrietta
came scurrying towards them. Her mob-cap and matching
apron were fluttering in the breeze and she was very much out
of breath.

With squeals of joy, her five babies ran forward to meet her.

"Hello, my dears!" she said, giving each one a friendly sniff.
"I hope I wasn't gone too long!"

"Hmph!" snorted Mr Badger, and disappeared through his
front doorway to get on with his nap.

"Where have you been?" squeaked Pippin the Squirrel.
"We've all been very worried about you!"

"Let her get her breath back," said Amanda Mole. "Come
inside and have a nice cup of nettle tea, Henrietta, and then
tell us all about it."

Everyone went into Amanda's dimly-lit parlour and
Amanda put the kettle on.

"Now then," she said, when everyone had been given a cup
of tea. "Tell us all about it, Henrietta."

Henrietta smoothed down her apron, adjusted her mob-cap,
and prepared to speak. Rosemary Rabbit and her sister
Amelia twitched their noses in excitement, waiting for the
story.

"It was like this," said Henrietta.

"Like what?" asked Pippin, unable to contain his curiosity.

"Like I'm going to tell you," said Henrietta.

"Stop interrupting, Pippin," said Amelia Rabbit, nervously.

"Sorry," said Pippin.

Henrietta began again.

"I was on my way to the Treetops Supermarket because Amanda had run out of Earwig Preserve," said Henrietta, "when I heard a lot of humans playing in a garden nearby. Well, where there are humans there are sometimes saucers of bread and milk, so I pushed through the hedge and you'll never believe what I saw!"

"What?" breathed everyone.

"Tables laid out with all kinds of food and drink, and a big cake burning up in the middle; and a baby human in a white shawl was being admired by a lot of people. There wasn't any bread and milk, though," reflected Henrietta, sadly. "But it was a sort of party, especially for the baby. It was a lovely cake, even though it was on fire."

"Fancy burning a cake! What a waste!" said Rosemary to Amelia.

"I know what it was," interrupted Charlie Crow. "It wasn't burning, it was candles. Humans put them on cakes for special occasions. They burn, but they don't burn the cake."

"Well, it looked like it," said Henrietta. "And then a man human came out with a thing they called a guitar and they all started singing and making nice noises; and I had an idea!"

"What?" asked everyone.

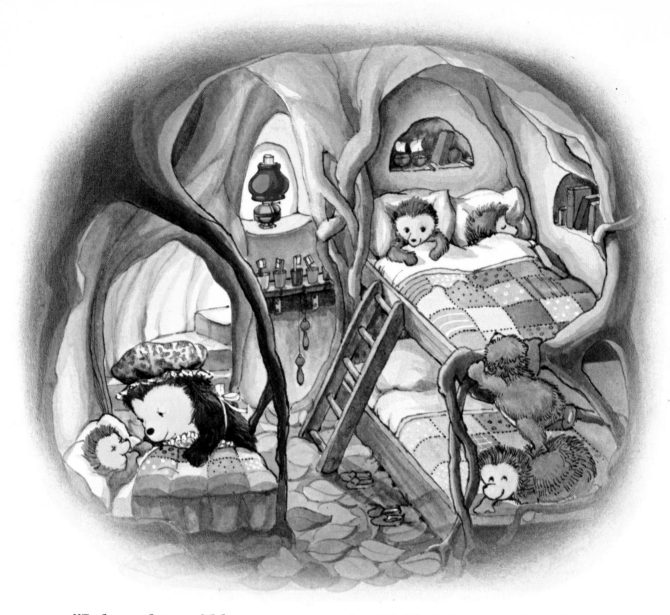

"I thought we'd have a party, too! I don't know why they were having one but the baby seemed to be very important, and as I've got five babies I shall hold a party for them. You must all come to it. We will have slug sandwiches and woodlouse jelly and beetle wine – I've got two big bottles of it – and I shall make a cake to burn."

"Or perhaps we could eat it, instead of burning it," suggested Pippin, hopefully. "Will there be nuts?"

"There'll be everything anyone wants to eat," Henrietta said. "Come to my house tomorrow afternoon at five o'clock!"

Henrietta took her babies home and put them to bed, telling them that if they went to sleep quickly, then tomorrow, and the party, would come all the quicker. Then she set to work, and because hedgehogs like night-time the best, she worked through the night until the sun rose on the new day.

Her little kitchen steamed with the heat from her oven and,

all around, on every one of her working surfaces, stood a tray of biscuits and cakes, all with pink and white icing. There were jellies and earthworm straws and, best of all, a magnificent iced cake.

"What a pity I have no candles," thought Henrietta. "Never mind, it looks lovely. Now I shall sleep before the guests arrive."

She slept all day, and woke just in time to lick her spines into shape and to clean up her babies before there was a knocking on the door.

When Henrietta opened it she found all her friends on the doorstep, their arms full of presents.

Henrietta squealed with delight and showed them the way into her front room.

"Charlie has found out what the humans' party was for," said Pippin. "Tell her, Charlie!"

"I flew back to see for myself," said Charlie. "And when I'd perched in a tree in their garden I heard one human say to the others 'Thank you for coming to our baby's christening party, and for all his lovely presents'."

"Rosemary and I asked Wise Owl what a christening party was," said Amelia. "We were a bit scared to ask but we plucked up the courage, and he told us that it's held to wish the baby well, and that the baby has godparents among his parents' friends who promise to look after him."

"So we're all going to be godparents to your babies," said Mr Badger.

"Oh, how lovely," said Henrietta. "Thank you."

There was one more surprise for Henrietta. As it got dark, and they could no longer see to play games in the garden,

Charlie flew to the gate and gave a loud croak.

Suddenly the path was filled with a scurrying of little footsteps and a darting of tiny bright lights.

"It's the glow-worms," squealed the baby hedgehogs.

The glow-worms ran on to the christening cake and stood in

groups, one on top of another. They glowed so brightly that Henrietta cried out in delight.

"Why," she said. "They look just like candles!"

Then the glow-worms did a dance, rearranging themselves in beautiful patterns all over the top of the cake. Everyone clapped when it was over, and the glow-worms bowed, then ran away before anyone could eat them by mistake among the icing.

"Thank you, Charlie and everyone," said Henrietta. "It's been a lovely party."

The Missing Mob~cap

Henrietta Hedgehog was in a terrible fluster one morning. Her five babies watched as she ran from one side of the garden to another, and then in and out of their house, without once stopping to sit down.

"What can be the matter?" they whispered to each other. "We'll be late for school if mother doesn't take us soon."

At last Henrietta stopped running around and looked hard at her five children.

"Have you hidden it, you naughty little dears?" she asked.

"Hidden what, Mother?" asked the baby hedgehogs.

"My mob-cap!" said Henrietta. "The one that matches this apron. I had it yesterday, I know I did."

"You didn't have it when you collected us from school, Mother," said Henry, who was the cleverest of the baby hedgehogs. "I thought you must have left it at home because it was so windy."

"Well, now!" said Henrietta. "There's a thing! I put it on to

come to meet you. The wind must have blown it away without me noticing."

The two youngest hedgehogs giggled suddenly, because they remembered how cross their mother had been when they had mislaid their school mittens the week before; but Henrietta took no notice. She was too upset at losing her mob-cap.

"Never mind," she said, sadly. "I shall have to buy another

piece of material and some elastic from Amanda Mole, and make another. Such a waste of money, though, with all of you needing things for school these days."

On the way back from taking the children to school, Henrietta had a surprise.

She was walking past the farmer's field on the edge of
Greenglades Wood when, through a gap in the hedge, she saw
a scarecrow.

Now Henrietta, along with all the other woodland creatures
except the birds, knew that this scarecrow was only a large
sort of doll, put there to scare the birds away from the crop

growing in the field. So she was not surprised to see the scarecrow . . . but she was very surprised indeed to see what had been placed on the scarecrow's head.

It was a flowery-patterned mob-cap, just like the material of

Henrietta's apron. In fact, Henrietta realised with a gasp, it was her mob-cap.

With an angry shout Henrietta scurried across the field, up and down over the ploughed lumps of soil, until, out of breath, she arrived at the scarecrow's feet.

"You . . . you wicked man!" she shouted. "How dare you steal my mob-cap! Give it back to me at once. At once, do you hear?"

Then it struck her that she was being very silly. Of course the scarecrow couldn't hear. He wasn't a real person!

Someone must have found her mob-cap lying on the ground and given it to the scarecrow, thought Henrietta. Well, now she was going to get it back.

There was a snuffling noise behind her and she turned to see Alfie Fieldmouse watching her with his bright button eyes.

"Hello, Henrietta!" said Alfie. "You're a long way from home in the Greenglades Wood, aren't you?"

Henrietta explained why she was there.

"You'll have to climb up and get it yourself," said Alfie. "Or

I'll try for you, if you like."

"Oh, Alfie, how kind of you!" said Henrietta. So the little fieldmouse began to climb up the scarecrow's leg.

He had not clambered very far up the leg when he slid down again. He tried and he tried, but he was not strong enough to climb to the scarecrow's head.

Henrietta tried, but she was too stout to get far. Each time, she fell down again, out of breath.

They were just wondering what to do when they heard a loud cawing sound behind them. They turned round and there

was Charlie Crow, sitting on the gatepost at the edge of the field, flapping his wings in a very agitated manner.

"Come away! It's dangerous! Dangerous!" he yelled.

"Birds!" said Alfie Fieldmouse in a disgusted way. "Silly creatures!"

Henrietta ran across the field to Charlie.

"Oh, Charlie, you're just the person I need," she said, happily. "You see, I lost my mob-cap yesterday and someone has put it on the scarecrow's head. Alfie and I have tried to climb up to get it back but it is too hard for us; but you could fly to the head of the scarecrow and take it away in your beak. The mob-cap, I mean," she added.

"Henrietta!" gasped Charlie. He had gone a funny shade of green. "I can't do that! Don't you know that birds are terrified of scarecrows? That's why farmers put them into fields."

"But, Charlie, there's nothing to be afraid of," said Henrietta. "It won't hurt you – it's only a toy person!"

Charlie looked sad, but he shook his head.

"I'm sorry, Henrietta," he said. "I'm just afraid, like all the other birds."

Henrietta sighed, but she managed to smile at Charlie.

"Never mind, Charlie," she said. "Everyone's scared of something. I'll go home and make a new mob-cap for myself."

Charlie watched her little figure trudging sadly off towards the wood, and thought of all the nice things she had done for him.

Screwing up his courage, he looked up at his enemy, the scarecrow.

"I'll be brave!" he told himself. "For Henrietta!"

With a sudden burst of energy he swooped across the field towards the scarecrow, and plucked the mob-cap from its head as he flew over it.

Landing in front of Henrietta he dropped the mob-cap at her feet.

"Charlie! You did it!" cried Henrietta joyfully.

Charlie proudly fluffed up his feathers.

"Yes, I did, didn't I?" he said, happily. "There was nothing to it, really. I don't know what I was frightened of. And I'll tell you something, Henrietta. I'm going back to sit on his head!"

He flew off again, cawing loudly, and landed on top of the scarecrow's straw hair. He flapped his wings and jumped up and down.

The noise brought all the woodland creatures out to the edge of the field. Pippin the squirrel was there first, then Rosemary and Amelia Rabbit, and even Amanda Mole left her shop and stood there blinking in the sunlight. They all cheered and

clapped when Henrietta explained what Charlie had done.

Charlie flew back to join them and they all said what a fine fellow he was.

"Thank you, Charlie," said Henrietta.

"Thank you, Henrietta," said Charlie. "I won't run away from things ever again."

Henrietta's Loaf of Bread

One day in Greenglades Wood, Amanda Mole got a message from her brother Herbert.

"He's twisted his ankle, Amanda," said the little mouse who had brought the message. "Please could you come over and help him?"

"Of course," said Amanda. "I'll shut up the shop and come over straight away."

When the little mouse had gone, Amanda remembered that Henrietta Hedgehog hadn't been in for her loaf of herb bread.

"Bother," said Amanda. "Never mind, I'll leave it with someone." She peeped out of the shop doorway but there was nobody in sight.

"Isn't that just the way?" said Amanda to herself. "There's never anyone around when you want them." She decided to leave the bread on Mr Badger's step as no-one would tamper with a loaf they thought belonged to Mr Badger.

She went into her back room and wrote a note on a piece of paper.

"Dear Henrietta," said the note. "Have been called away. Your bread is beside Mr Badger's front door."

She wrapped the bread up in several pieces of paper and tied it up with string. Then she pinned the note to the front

door of the shop, left the bread by Mr Badger's front door, and set off to visit her brother.

It so happened that Mr Badger had been having a sleepless day, and had gone out for a walk to try to tire himself out so that he could have a deep afternoon sleep. Badgers, you know,

go out at night and sleep during the day. Well, Mr Badger came home just after Amanda went out.

"Ho, hum!" he yawned to himself. "That walk has made me really sleepy. Oh . . . what's this?"

He had fallen over the loaf of bread beside his front doorstep.

"That's a loaf of bread," he thought, sniffing hard at it. "But it can't be for me because I haven't ordered any. Perhaps someone dropped it by mistake. I know – it could have been Alfie Fieldmouse. He's got a big family and he has to pass my doorstep on his way home from Amanda's shop. I'll take it to him."

Now, if Mr Badger hadn't been so sleepy he would have realised that Alfie Fieldmouse could never eat a big loaf like that, even with the help of his family, and Alfie could never have carried such a big loaf all the way home. However, Mr Badger was thinking of his bed and the nice snooze he was going to have, so he hurried all the way to Alfie's with the loaf.

When Alfie answered the door, Mr Badger told him that he'd found his loaf of bread for him and then he ran home as fast as he could, climbed under his eiderdown and fell asleep.

Alfie looked at the big parcel, and scratched his head.

"We can't have that lying around here," said Mrs Fieldmouse, crossly. "Before we know it there'll be all kinds of

people scavenging around on our doorstep wanting some of it. You and the boys must take it back at once before that nasty stoat and weasel gang get a sniff of it."

Alfie always did as his wife told him, so he called his five strong sons and between them they got the parcel on to their shoulders and scurried off back into the wood with it.

After a while the youngest son called "Stop! Stop!" and Alfie and the others stopped. The loaf rolled off their backs and landed against a tree.

"Where are we taking it, Dad?" asked the youngest son, who was also the brightest.

"I don't know, son," said Alfie. "Your mother just wanted it out of the way."

"Well, it's out of the way now, isn't it?" said the youngest

son. So Alfie clapped him on the back and told him he was a clever lad, and then they all went home to tea.

Meanwhile, Henrietta Hedgehog had called to collect her herb bread from Amanda Mole's shop. She was most surprised to see that the door was shut, and she could not think what

had become of her loaf. She did not see the note which Amanda had left because it had blown away in the breeze.

"Oh dear," she said. "And I was going to make slug paste sandwiches for supper."

She walked home again, wondering what she could give her

babies instead. She was so busy thinking about this that she did not hear Pippin the Squirrel calling good-day to her.

Pippin didn't stop to ask her what was wrong, because he was in a hurry to get home. He had made a Dundee cake for his tea, and he couldn't wait to eat the nuts which decorated the top.

He arrived at his house to find a large parcel at the bottom of the tree. You see, he lived in the very tree that Alfie and his sons had stopped at, and Henrietta's loaf of bread was resting beside it. Pippin nibbled away a corner of the paper with his teeth and peeped inside.

"Why, it's a loaf of bread!" he said. "Someone must have delivered it to me by mistake. Perhaps it was Rosemary and Amelia Rabbit."

So he picked it up and took it to their burrow.

"Why, how very kind of you to bring us a loaf of bread," said Amelia. "You are a very kind squirrel, Pippin."

Pippin didn't like to say that he wasn't a very kind squirrel at all, and that the loaf of bread wasn't a real present, so he said nothing.

"It's so nicely wrapped, too," said Rosemary, not noticing the corner which Pippin had chewed away. "Will you stay for tea?"

"No, thank you," said Pippin, who didn't like the salad sandwiches which the two rabbit ladies had for tea. "I must be going. I've got things to do."

Rosemary and Amelia waved him goodbye.

"I didn't like to tell him we'd got two loaves just baked," said Rosemary.

"It would have been rude," said Amelia. "But, sister, what are we going to do with three loaves?"

"I'll take it round to Henrietta," said Rosemary. "She's just

come in, and with her big family she'll be able to use it, I'm sure."

When Rosemary opened Henrietta's door and called "Coo-eee!" an amazing noise hit her ears. All the baby

hedgehogs were crying because they had wanted slug paste sandwiches for tea.

"What a terrible noise!" thought Rosemary, and out loud she said, "I've just brought you a loaf of bread, Henrietta! I

won't stop!" Then she ran away as fast as she could to the peace and quiet of her own home.

Henrietta was delighted. She picked up the loaf of bread and started cutting it up to make the sandwiches. All the little hedgehogs dried their tears and smiled again, because they knew they would be getting their favourite tea after all.

So neither Henrietta, nor Amanda Mole, ever knew how many people had had the chance of eating that loaf of bread before it came to its rightful owner!